THE LANGUAGE OF CAT

AND OTHER POEMS

I.M. Elizabeth Quinn

JANETTA OTTER-BARRY BOOKS

First published in Great Britain in 2011 by
Frances Lincoln Children's Books, 4 Torriano Mews,
Torriano Avenue, London NW5 2RZ
www.franceslincoln.com

A catalogue record for this book is available from the British Library.

ISBN 978-1-84780-167-8

Illustrated with pen and pencil

Set in Charlotte Book

Printed in Croydon, Surrey, UK by CPI Bookmarque Ltd.
in January 2011

1 3 5 7 9 8 6 4 2

THE LANGUAGE OF CAT

AND OTHER POEMS

Poems by
RACHEL ROONEY

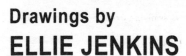

Drawings by
ELLIE JENKINS

F

FRANCES LINCOLN
CHILDREN'S BOOKS

Contents

Who?

Who cast the **P** from a spell
sold it for profit as sell,
then kept what was left
in a locked letter chest?

And who sucked the **O** from a hoop,
hopped off with that loop
which she balanced for fun
on the tip of her tongue?

Who stole the **E** from a cheat
in the street when they met for a chat,
slipped her hand in a bag
and made off with the swag?

Then who plucked the **T** from a thorn,
carved an ivory pen out of horn
and dipped it in ink...
Well, who do you think did that?

The Language of Cat

Teach me the language of Cat;
the slow-motion blink, that crystal stare,
a tight-lipped purr and a wide-mouthed hiss.
Let me walk with a saunter, nose in the air.

Teach my ears the way to ignore
names that I'm called. May they only twitch
to the distant shake of a boxful of biscuits,
the clink of a fork on a china dish.

Teach me that vanishing trick
where dents in cushions appear, and I'm missed.
Show me the high-wire trip along fences
to hideaway places, that no-one but me knows exist.

Don't teach me Dog,
all eager to please; that slobbers, yaps and begs for a pat,
that sits when told by its owner, that's led on a lead.
No, not that. Teach me the language of Cat.

Nought to Nine

A ring made of gold, a doughnut and hole,
something that's nothing that's easy to roll.

A periscope raised, a walking stick,
the cut of a cake and a candle's new wick.

A swan on a lake, a nun knelt in prayer,
an FA Cup handle raised in the air.

The pout of a mouth, a bird flying over,
a bra on a line, two leaves of a clover.

A neatly pressed ribbon, a kite without string,
the nose of a witch and an arm in a sling.

The hand of a pirate, a flat-headed snake,
an apple divided, the latch on a gate.

A teardrop to wipe, a cherry and stalk,
the speech mark to use when your words start to talk.

Half a triangle, a fox's ear tip,
an arrow, an arm of a hand on a hip.

Balancing balls and a circular kiss,
a hoop with a waist and a rope in a twist.

A hook in a curtain, chameleon's tongue,
the whistle to blow when this poem is done.

Sonnet for a Sphere

Take an apple. Chop it into quarters.
Count out three. These represent the lakes
that nestle inside countries, all the snaking
rivers joined with seas – the blue that's water.

Put them aside. This last remaining slice
stands for the land. Divide it into eight.
Discard the barren: the distant icy waste,
the thirsty desert, rocky unreached heights.

What's left? Just one last sliver of a sphere.
Unpeel its skin. Hold up that patch of green
between your thumb and fingertip. It's here
the soil is rich and seeds take root. The crops
we need to harvest, where our livestock feed
are all in this. Be careful now – don't drop it.

O the wonderful shape of an O

o see the wonderful shape of an o it's just a continuous flow there's no other letter that's rounder or better with neither a stop nor a g

Gravity

If it wasn't for Earth's
gravitational pull
then objects would float up
and skies would be full
of ripe conkers, bombs, cow dung,
those pencils we lose
from coat pockets, high jumpers
like large kangaroos,
confetti, leaves, litter
a melee of fruit,
all those sticks thrown for puppies
and those footballs we boot.

Imagine: this planet a much tidier place.
But think of that mess up in space.

Icarus

Icarus
was thick because
he ignored the basic facts:
the sun's hot, it melts wax.

Unfair

She picked the fight
but now she cries.
I know I'm right.
She's telling lies

but now she cries
for sympathy.
She's telling lies,
and he blames me.

For sympathy
she dabs her face,
and he blames me.
I'm in disgrace.

She dabs her face,
she gets a hug.
I'm in disgrace,
she's looking smug.

She gets a hug,
I want to cry.
She's looking smug
I'm sure that's why

I want to cry.
I know I'm right.
I'm sure that's why
she picked the fight.

Signature

First, he wrote it in pencil, on paper.
Next, on a desk with a felt tip. Later
etched into doors with a sharpened knife.
Robert Ian Price

Found on billboards, bridges, buses,
public toilets, underpasses.
If he's written it once, you've seen it twice.
Robert Ian Price

Dreaming of cheques and autographs
he traced his name on steamed-up glass,
wet sandy beaches, ponds of ice.
Robert Ian Price

Hired a plane; learnt how to fly.
Sprayed his initials in a cloudless sky.
Dizzy with fame, but not so clever.
R.I.P. Forever.

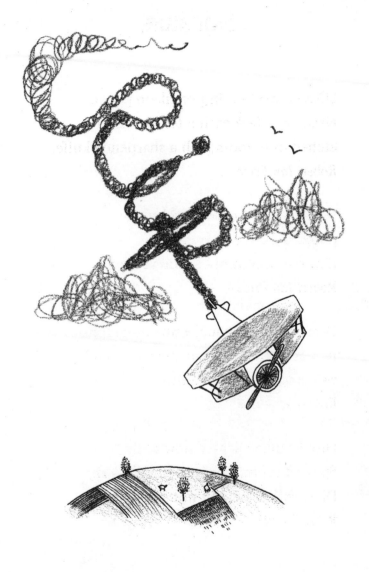

Russian Doll

All you see is outside me: my painted smile,
the rosy-posy shell, the fluttery eyes.
A butter-won't-melt-in-my-mouth-type me

But inside there's another me, bored till playtime.
The wasting paper, daytime dreamer.
A can't-be-bothered-sort-of me.

And inside there's another me, full of cheek.
The quick, slick joker with a poking tongue.
A class-clown-funny-one-of me

And inside there's another me who's smaller, scared.
The scurrying, worrying, yes miss whisperer.
A wouldn't-say-boo-to-a-goosey me

And inside there's another me, all cross and bothered.
The scowling hot-head, stamping feet.
A didn't-do-it-blameless me.

And inside there's another me, forever jealous
who never gets enough, compared.
A grass-is-always-greener me.

And deepest down, kept secretly
a tiny, solid skittle doll.
The girl that hides inside of me.

She Said

I caught an object, asked it *What?*
Oh dear, it mumbled, *I forgot.*

I chose a place and asked it *Where?*
But all it sighed was *Here and there.*

I made a time and asked it *When?*
It whispered weakly *Now and then.*

I found a reason, asked it *Why?*
It's just because I heard it cry.

I saw a way and asked it *How?*
It shrugged. *Nobody knows that now.*

I met a person, asked them *Who?*
The answer, she said, *lies with you.*

Three Monkeys

See No Evil didn't see
what Hear No Evil did.
He ran off to the jungle,
closed his eyes and hid.

Hear No Evil didn't hear
what See No Evil said.
He put his hands upon his ears
and hummed a tune instead.

Speak No Evil didn't speak.
He didn't shout or tell.
But there are other monkeys.
(And that is just as well.)

The Thing I Can't Have

The thing I can't have is the best thing,
I find myself wanting it more.
I know I can't get it
but cannot forget it.
Some feelings are hard to ignore.

It's the chocolate I wanted with nuts in.
It's winning the Champions Cup.
It's that lucky pink ticket.
It's taking the wicket.
It's the place in the queue lining up.

It's being the eldest – or youngest.
It's the whisper of words I can't hear.
It's the passenger seat.
It's the smell of a sweet.
It's the dangerous ride on the pier.

The thing I can't have is the best thing
and although it is sure to annoy,
there's something in wanting
the thing I can't have
that's a feeling I almost enjoy.

The Making of
the Gingerbread Man

I made you mine. Your name was whispered
softly sifted with the flour, ginger.
Cut butter slipped like silent kisses
in the mix, and greased my fingers.

Sweet with sugar, syrup, wet with egg
I kneaded you. Your dough flesh rolled
and gently pressed to shape, your arms and legs
outstretched. I gave you buttons, eyes, a nose.

I scored a thumbnail smile. And smiling back
slid you warm inside to bake. Waited.
Salivated. Placed you on the rack
to cool and turned away. Then you escaped.

Too quick for me, you ran. All I caught
were taunting words, a blurred and laughing face.
Left chewing hard, round biscuits, lost in thought
I wonder what became of you; your taste.

Reflection

Look to the mirror:
> there's a girl you think you know.

Look to the river:
> all the places she could go.

Look to the glass:
> and her wide, transparent eyes.

Look to the pond:
> note the way the waters lie.

Look to the spoon:
> in a topsy-turvy world.

Look to the moon:
> see it smiling at the girl.

Post

A queen in a palace, slumped on a throne,
surrounded by servants but all alone.
Heavy with handshakes, bunches of flowers,
jewels, crowns, grinning for hours.
Fed up, bored, decided to quit
so used her head and some royal spit.
Flicked through a book, picked a random address:
5, The High Street, Inverness.
Stuck her face on a card, destination beneath.
Does one fancy a swap, Ms Morag Mackeith?
Posted it off, didn't delay.
Saw herself landing, first class next day
with an inky tattoo (yesterday's date)
on a mat. Sat back. Couldn't wait.

That night she dreamt of burger and chips,
a part-time job with lunchtime kips,
allotment keys and charity shops,

queuing for loos, bingo, bus stops,
neighbours, backyards, The Christmas Club,
a seat by the fire in her local pub.
She tore up her diary, started to pack.

But Morag Mackeith never wrote back.

80% of People Prefer Chips to Poems

Eighty per cent of people like chips.
Ten per cent choose rice.
Four per cent are partial to naan
and three say noodles are nice.

One per cent think batter best.
One simply refuses tea.
And one per cent of all the rest
devours poetry.

Mermaid's Lament

I've had enough of perching on rocks
stinking of fish, waiting for sailors
to pass by and fall in love.

I want to swim away to shore,
stand up on my own two feet and walk
tall across dry land.

I want go disco dancing with mates,
look great in my high-heeled stilettos
and tight blue jeans.

I want to pedal hard up a steep hill,
then legs outstretched, freewheel down
just for the fun of it.

I want to be a striker, take a penalty
and score the golden goal, perform cartwheels
to a roaring crowd.

Or simply lounge on the beach in a twin-set bikini,
paint my toenails, and watch the fishermen
emptying out their nets.

Just Her and the Poet

Just her, a lamp, an open book.
An open book, the glow of the page.
The glow of the page, its inky print.
Its inky print, those thinking lines.
Those thinking lines – a poem's face.
A poem's face like the man in the moon.
The man in the moon like a poem's face.
A poem's face – those thinking lines.
Those thinking lines, its inky print.
Its inky print, the glow of the page.
The glow of the page, an open book.
Just an open book, a lamp and the poet.

Calculation

Love plus love is addition.
Times love is a love multiplied.
Taken away, it's a minus.
Love into itself, a divide.

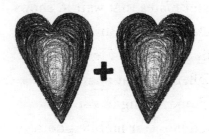

This Modern Monster

This monster is a high-tech beast
man-made, an import from Japan.
A slim-line foe, no fur or slime.
Its skin, lightweight titanium.
And on its flip-top swivelling head
an eye to spy on you. It knows
the paths you tread. It can communicate:
transmit, long-distance, video
to monster mates that wait in shops
while scheming silently by text.
Next thing, instead of feeling fear
you've fallen for that charmed ring tone.
And find one sitting in your palm
a dreaded monster mobile phone
demanding to be fed.

Predictive Text

Hope is a hose.
Blood is alone.
A rope is a rose
and a bond is a bone.

Hips are a hiss.
and a shard is a phase.
Lips are a kiss
and a page is a rage.

Plaques are a plaster.
Crops are a cross.
A mark is a mask
and a poet is soft.

Charm Bracelet

And an anchor,
just in case.

This one's a boat
to sail the seas.

Here's a compass
pointing North.

And this, a star
to shimmer.

An angel
to keep me safe.

Here's a cat
for company.

This, a book
to hold my thoughts.

And a fish,
if we wish for dinner.

Crossing the Rockery

I choose an angled rock
that rises like a mountain's spine
from the undergrowth.
Uncurl a naked heel to toe
across its sharp ridge.
Feel a dig into sole
as I take the weight of me;
my other foot hovering
over jungle and dry stone.
Now, I am in Africa,
my own private tribe
and I'm crossing the rockery, barefoot.
I am strong.
I am brave.
I will conquer this continent.

Sir!

I just want to please Sir.
Please, Sir. Please, Sir. Please.

Why don't you choose me, Sir.
Me, Sir. Me, Sir. Me.

I'm down on my knees, Sir.
Knees, Sir. Knees, Sir. Knees.

The answer is Three, Sir.
Three, Sir. Three, Sir. Three.

I'm clever you see, Sir.
See, Sir. See, Sir. See.

But now I must leave, Sir.
Leave, Sir. Leave, Sir. Leave.

I'm going to Miss, Sir.
Miss Sir. Miss Sir.

Miss!

Three Goldfish

ONE
I was just messing,
practising passes.
Nobody told me
how breakable glass is.

TWO
You needed fresh water,
but then I forgot
that C stands for Cold
and H stands for Hot.

THREE
I didn't feed you.
Nor did my brother.
Both of us thought
You were fed by the other.

The Poem and the Poet

The **c**hicken comes before the **e**gg,
a **f**rog before its **s**pawn.
The **p**lant must come before the **s**eed
and **d**eers before their **f**awn
But **m**ums come after **b**oys and **g**irls,
(perhaps you didn't know it).
So can you tell me which comes first,
the **poem** or the **poet** ?

Ig-pay Atin-lay

Ig-pay Atin-lay is-hay ite-quay easy-hay
En-whay ou-yay earn-lay e-thay ules-ray.
I-hay ink-thay ey-thay ould-shay onsider-cay
eaching-tay it-hay in-hay ools-schay.

Pig Latin is quite easy
when you learn the rules.
I think they should consider
teaching it in schools.

(Translation)

Bring and Buy

Sold my mother at the Summer Fayre
to a year 3 kid. Good buy.
Six quid. A bargain at half the price...
didn't think twice, I swear.
Found a great mum going spare:
big boots, spiked hair – dyed pink.
So walked her back to mine. Like mates,
our footsteps fell in synch.

Dined on take-aways, lay in bed
but fed-up quick with fast food,
mess and being late for Miss,
took her away instead.
Swapped her for another mother.
This one smarter: slick
side-parting, high-heeled shoes, posh skirt.
Looked like an advert. Tricked.

Should have guessed the rest: the muesli,
manners, star charts, tests,
In bed by eight and no buts. Please,
she's got to leave. Can't wait.
Then met my real mum,
good as new and maybe better.
Told that kid in year 3, when he's through
I'll pay out a tenner to get her.

Recycling

A word is used often, over time.
Used, a word is often over.
Time is a used word.
Over used, a word
is a word
often used
wastefully.

Boast

I've got a friend who swallowed a stopwatch
in three minutes and forty two and a half seconds.

I've got a friend who swallowed a lamp post.
He lives down our street.

I've got a friend who swallowed a DVD.
I've seen her do it loads of times.

I've got a friend who swallowed a wide-screen T.V.
Now she's famous.

I've got a friend who swallowed a fence.
He's always round our house.

I've got a friend who swallowed a lie-detector.
Honest!

A Greengage is a Type of Plum
(A true story)

A greengage is a type of plum.
I know this fact because my mum
brought home a sack full of the stuff.
'Well you can never have enough
of fresh fruit for the family,'
she said, 'especially when it's free.'

That night we ate them ripe and raw,
then finding there were plenty more,
decided that she ought to try
a recipe for greengage pie.
And as the sack was hardly dented,
other puddings she invented.
Crumble, jams and Roly Poly
bakes and cakes were served up solely
for our pleasure. But no thanks
were given from her hungry ranks.
Worse than this, we soon grew tired
of that taste, once quite admired.

On day eight to our displeaure
after dinner, in great measure
we received, against our wishes
stewed greengages served in dishes.
My father, not a man to grumble
was overheard to softly mumble
'Oh no, it's not those things again.'
My mother didn't answer. Then
stood up, and walking to his chair,
she raised his serving in the air,
and calmly without warning tipped
it from above. The warm plums dripped
all sweet and sticky from his brow,
upon the table, dishless now.

Mum returned back to her seating
and resumed her silent eating.
Dad went to wash, while leaving us
to eat our pudding without fuss.

There is no moral to this tale
of greed or gratitude or scale.
These things apply, but my point is,
that I'll remember in a quiz
this fructal fact, (all thanks to mum).
A greengage is a type of plum.

Growing

Shoes pinch tighter, house shrinks smaller.
Shadows taller, darkness lighter.

Sleep comes later, week ends quicker.
Books thicker, journeys greater.

Tests loom nearer, questions tougher.
Waves rougher, skies clearer.

Past grows longer. Getting older,
bigger, bolder, brighter, stronger.

Halfway

Halfway between the big bang and a black hole.
Halfway between an atom and deep space.
Halfway between the sea-bed and the summit.
Half-wishing I was in a different place.

Halfway between the night-light and the neon.
Halfway between the rap and nursery rhyme.
Halfway between this minute and the future.
Half-hoping it could be another time.

Halfway between a penny and a cheque book.
Halfway between the driving seat and pram.
Halfway between the walker and the high-heel.
Half-knowing who on earth I think I am.

Counting Days

It's been six days, I've kept my silence well.
I give a yes or no, a stunted phrase.
My mother sighs, I don't think she can tell
the anger's gone. I'm simply counting days.

I didn't wipe the crumbs up. Words were said,
then later screamed across the bedroom door.
What started off as fussing over bread
became a full-blown mother-daughter war.

The bread's gone stale. My mother cannot wait.
She asks me why I'm choosing not to speak.
I hesitate and shrug. I calculate
that I can hold my silence for a week.

Driving Home

I hold this shell against my ear.
Inside, a wave that sucks the shore,
music drifting from the pier,
a tapping spade, a seagull's call.

Listen, sea-shell. Can you hear
my heart sink slowly with the sun,
the rolling of a salty tear
and an engine's sleepy hum?

Mirror

One was beautiful, silken hair to her waist
and dutiful, kept it neatly in place.
Please and **Thanks** were words she'd use.
Cleared up the dishes, polished her shoes.

One was wild, a mop of woolly tresses,
barefoot, grubby, never wore dresses.
Snot on her sleeve, she spat and swore
ranted and raged, then slammed the door.

They stared at each other, the same green eyes
and what they saw they recognised.
You're me! said the first **How do you do?**
Watch out! said the other **I'm You.**

Acceleration

A toddler teetered high on a hill.
Took his first step, and another until
the walk took a trip, split a second
and started to run.

Just for the fun of it, trampled on time.
The length that it took for a nursery rhyme
to finish a book. The hush of a finger.
One minute.

He ran with the wind on his back through a blaze
of goodnights, wake-ups, in between days.
Skipped across weekends, teachers,
overgrown shoes.

Widening his stride, he cruised over seasons.
Joined up the years with a string of good reasons.
Zero to Eighty Three.
He was there in a shake.

Braking, he couldn't recall getting older.
Called it a day. Glanced over his shoulder.
A growing snowball of memories
rolling his way.

What I Really Mean
(A found poem)

I didn't say she stole my money.
(But someone said she did.)

I *didn't* say she stole my money.
(I really, really didn't.)

I didn't **say** she stole my money.
(Pehaps I gave a hint.)

I didn't say *she* stole my money.
(But someone must have done it.)

I didn't say *stole* my money.
(I think she might have hidden it.)

I didn't say she stole *my* money.
(But she did take someone else's.)

I didn't say she stole my *money.*
(I said she stole my glasses.)

Fishing

I feel it, first as a stir,
turning deep in the murky water.
Surfaces up for air, a twitch
on the lake in my head.
A flip, and it disappears.

Wait for it. Let myself settle
close to the edge, my reflection and me.
Next ripple, a gentle skim and a dip
holds the weight of a thought
in the drag of my net.

Raising the pole, bent heavy,
my catch thrashes hard. Through the reeds
I can glimpse a glitter of skin.
Won't let it go now.
I have this idea.

Hauled out and tipped in a tub,
I'm watching it flap; its mouthing pout,
that eye that stares defiantly back.
A sizeable fish. How big?
As big as a poem. See!

Defending the Title

I am the word juggler.
I juggle the words
like swords.
I slice sense
with poetic licence.

I am the letter mover
the metre lover.
Like rhyme
I time this
for poetic justice.

I am the brain rattler.
Shaking ideas
like dice.
A notion
in poetic motion.

I am the verse making
rule bending defender.
Beginner
and ender.
I am the champion.

Tornado

I knew a girl; a tornado
born on a storm.
Arrived in a whirl, with a thump
on the hospital floor.

Picked herself up, found her feet
but still she was reeling.
The world was a blur, off-kilter
and all she kept feeling

was dizzy and queasy and dazed.
To stop herself churning
she did what she needed to do
and carried on turning.

Like a coin, a top, a wheel,
the floss on a stick
or the drum of a washing machine
as it reaches its peak,

she spun faster. Her arms outstretched
like blades of a chopper.
She rose from this world into space.
Nothing on earth could stop her.

The Statue

He stands by day, plinth high.
Once real, important, maybe even kind.
Inviting the girl to climb.
Foot into stone into knee,
hand in iron hand,
she clasps onto him
for that last stretch up.
Here, now, giddy flesh
pressed against metal,
she's the biggest thing alive.
At night, he wakes in purple light
to see the girl, hurrying past
head to earth, breathing fast.
Alone.
As iron lifts from stone
she stops,
turns,
freezes him with her stare.

The Trouble is...

Like jigsaw pieces from a different box
Like faulty plugs that have a broken pin
Like some odd key that won't undo the locks
The trouble is... I don't fit in.
Like heavy black bin-bags to empty, or
Like muddy balls and boots when others shout
Like rinsed milk bottles lined up at the door
The trouble is... I am left out.
But unlike jigsaw pieces, plugs or keys
And all those other things I mentioned there,
I'm not an object, I can think and feel.
The trouble is... I just don't care.

Timetable

work work play work play work home

work work play work play work home

work work play work play work home

work work play work play work home

work work play work play work home

play play play play play play play

play play play play play home work

Elizabeth Quinn

There's a girl that we know called Elizabeth Quinn
Her eyes are too big and her skin's too thin.
So much to see. So much to feel.
Life is too large for her, life is too real.

She makes mountains from molehills, grows tired of the climb.
Is wary of whirlpools at the end of bath-time.
The lightning strike of a match sees her start
and the thunder in handclaps puts strain on her heart.

At daybreak she worries that nightime will fall.
Predicts the next earthquake from cracks in the wall.
We tell her to toughen up. Don't make a fuss.
Get a grip. Grin and bear it. Act something like us.

But she doesn't answer. Our voices are drowned
by the split of a raindrop hitting the ground,
the uncurl of petals, the sighing of bees,
the rustle of sunlight that falls through the trees.

With her heels to the sky, her chin in her palm
she's down in the meadow; quiet, calm.
Deep in the soft grass, enjoying the view
she's captured by cobwebs and dazzled by dew.

There's a girl that we know called Elizabeth Quinn
Her eyes are so big and her skin's so thin.
Too much to see. Too much to feel.
She lives her life large and she lives her life real.

On the Way Back

I collect my own good luck:
look out for yellow cars,
kick stones in drains, first time,
and touch the wooden-only gates
of houses passing by.
I'll be all right.
The lights have changed from green to red
before I count to ten.
And still the flashing man is bleeping
as I step up on the pavement.
I've made my own good luck.
I'm clutching fistfuls of the stuff.
Maybe this time there's just enough
to keep me safe
until this journey's over.

Bookmark

An open book: a girl slips in.
Delicate, dreamy, paper thin
and hungry. *Please may I begin?*
My two-dimensional twin.

We dine from left to right. Each line,
a trail of words. Her hand takes mine.
Everything will be just fine.
My sympathetic twin.

Sleep too, has got an appetite.
I close the book, dim down the light.
Identical in sheets of white.
Page 83. *Goodnight.*

The Edge of Things

I like to climb to the 85th floor,
the brink of a cliff, tall trees;
my skin against air.
Or standing below, look up
at myself as I'm teetering there.

I like to straddle the border, divided:
the right of me North, left South.
Or balance the line
walking steady and straight,
in nobody's land but mine.

I like to circle the crowd; run rings
and peer at them, all peering in.
Or out from this world
to the stitch of the stars,
eyes widening like pearls.

I like to be on the edge of things;
hear midnight's final strike
as I'm turning thirteen,
that moment I fall into sleep,
the start of a dream.

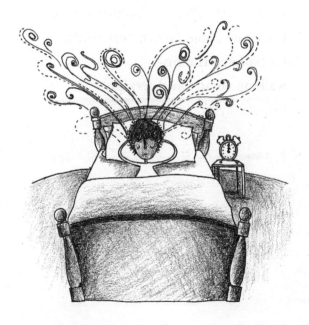

Take it

Take this poem, wrap its weight round a stone.
Bury it. Turn from the earth where it sits.
Let the words decompose, undisturbed.

Send it off from a sheer mountain's ridge,
folded inward, and stiffened with fear.
Let it dive with a cry from your hearing.

Hold it under an incoming wave
so the stain of its ink is sucked from the page.
Let it spill in the tide like a sin.

Set a match to it. Savour the lick of a flame
that swallows the dark that's swallowing it.
Let it burn to a pinched finger's tip.

Take this poem from out of my hands.
It's all I have left now to give.
Take it and do what you will with it.

Daisy's Answer

I asked her why she chose to stay,
disturbed by threats of churning blades,
footballs, dogs and sticks in play.
But she did not reply.

And as the shadows sank the day,
I turned and saw a daisy chain
and a smiling child. No need to say.
She slowly winked her eye.

Target

Aim higher than the clod of mud,
the thud in earth that's swallowed up,

the belly of a rusted can,
the clang of tin, unbalancing,

snails that cling to low flint walls,
the cracking of a hollow shell,

the plum upon a neighbour's tree,
a hush disturbed within its leaves,

and higher still than startled crows,
slanted attic windows, rows

of chimney stacks, church spires,
tower blocks. Aim higher.

Set sight between the blazing past
and unlit future of a star.

Aim now.

Question

If the sun was the size of a beach ball
and the earth was as large as a pea
and the moon as small as a peppercorn –
how tiny would we be?

How to Say Goodbye

With a hug, a shrug, a slap or kiss.
With cheers, or tears and promises.

In a letter, a text, by telephone.
In a crowd out loud or whispered alone.

From a waving hand, on land, at sea.
From the heart, the mouth, on the count of three.

To a teacher, passer-by, a friend.
Tomorrow, for now, until the end.

A word, in a poem, from me to you.
Adios. Farewell. Adieu.

RACHEL ROONEY trained as a special needs teacher and currently works with children with Autistic Spectrum Condition. She also teaches poetry workshops for West Sussex's Gifted and Talented Programme, and leads workshops in schools as a visiting poet. She has been shortlisted for the Belmont Poetry Prize, commended in the 2010 Escalator poetry competition, and 60 of her poems have been published in children's poetry anthologies. *The Language of Cat* is her first book of collected poems. She lives in Brighton.

MORE POETRY FROM
FRANCES LINCOLN CHILDREN'S BOOKS

978-1-84780-166-1 • PB • £5.99

An A-Z of animal poems with a difference!
Choose your favourite from Roger McGough's
witty and wicked menagerie.

"Classic Roger McGough" – *Guardian*

978-1-84780-168-5 • PB • £5.99

Perfect for younger children, these poems are fresh,
funny and brilliant for reading aloud.

"These poems are born out of years of visiting
infant classrooms. A real birthday party of words" –
Pie Corbett

978-1-84780-169-2 • PB • £5.99

From spooky legends to dreamy poems, teasers
and rhymes, expect the unexpected. A poetry adventure
waiting to happen!

"A poet with a powerful feeling for story and language" –
Carousel